I'm Growing Up!

My First Lost Tooth

Marigold Brooks

illustrated by
Joel Gennari

PowerKiDS press™

New York

Published in 2019 by The Rosen Publishing Group, Inc.
29 East 21st Street, New York, NY 10010

First Edition

Managing Editor: Nathalie Beullens-Maoui
Editor: Elizabeth Krajnik
Art Director: Michael Flynn
Book Design: Raúl Rodriguez
Illustrator: Joel Gennari

Cataloging-in-Publication Data

Names: Brooks, Marigold.
Title: My first lost tooth / Marigold Brooks.
Description: New York : PowerKids Press, 2019. | Series: I'm growing up! | Includes index.
Identifiers: LCCN ISBN 9781508167440 (pbk.) | ISBN 9781508167426 (library bound) |
ISBN 9781508167457 (6 pack)
Subjects: LCSH: Teeth–Juvenile fiction. | Tooth loss–Juvenile fiction. | Tooth Fairy (Legendary character)–Juvenile fiction.
Classification: LCC PZ7.B766 My 2019 | DDC [E]–dc23

Manufactured in the United States of America

CPSIA Compliance Information: Batch #CS18PK. For further information contact Rosen Publishing, New York, New York at 1-800-237-9932

Contents

A Loose Tooth   4

Baby Teeth   8

The Tooth Fairy   20

Words to Know   24

Index   24

My tooth is loose!
I can wiggle it with my finger.

I run downstairs to tell my grandma.

Grandma says I must be growing up!

7

Grandma says I have baby teeth.

As I grow up, my baby teeth will fall out.

9

What will I do without any teeth?

10

Grandma tells me not to worry.

When I lose a baby tooth
a new tooth will grow.

The new tooth
won't fall out.

I ask my grandma how to make
my tooth more loose.

She tells me to eat an apple.

I take a big bite out of a crunchy apple.

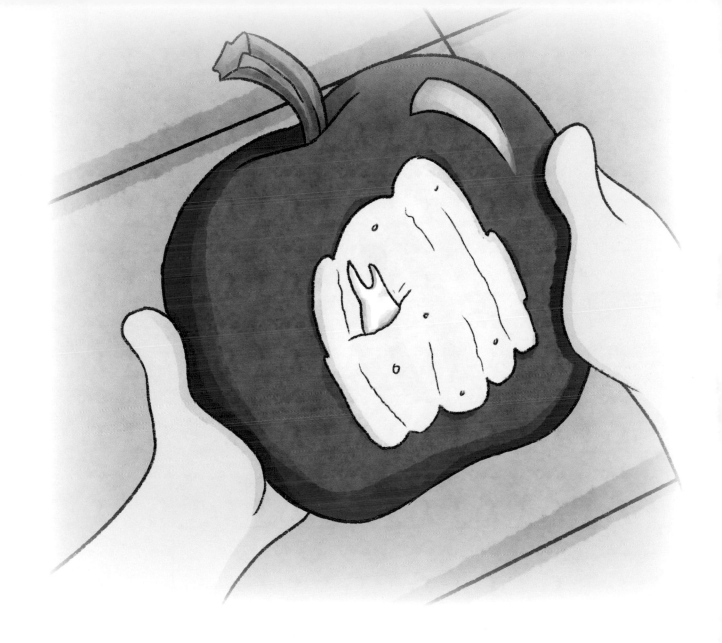

I feel my tooth get stuck!

My tooth came out!

Grandma gives me a special bag
to put it in.

Grandma says the tooth fairy will come take the tooth while I sleep.

I put the bag
under my pillow.

When I wake up
my tooth is gone! The tooth fairy
left behind a shiny new coin.

Words to Know

coin

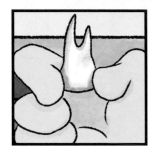

tooth

Index

B
baby tooth, 8, 9, 12

L
loose, 5, 14

N
new tooth, 12, 13

T
tooth fairy, 20, 23